270106130

DATE DUE			
OC 14 '85			
OC 21 '85			
OC 30 '85			
NO 6 '85			
NOV 20 '85			
NOV 27 '85			
DEC 4 '85			
DE 11 '85			
DE 12 '85			
DE 7 '94			

Mar   **844623**   9.95

Marney, D.
Just good friends

Just Good friends

Just Good Friends

Mar

9.95

by
Dean Marney

Addison-Wesley

Text Copyright © 1982 by Dean Marney
All Rights Reserved
Addison-Wesley Publishing Company, Inc.
Reading, Massachusetts 01867
Printed in the United States of America

ABCDEFGHIJK-DO-8987654321

Library of Congress Cataloging in Publication Data

Marney, Dean
  Just good friends.

  Summary: Thirteen-year-old Boyd is "just good
friends" with his two girl-friends, Marcia and
Lou, until he falls in love with Marcia.
  [1. Friendship—Fiction. 2. Interpersonal rela-
tions—Fiction] I. Title.
PZ7.M3459Ju   [Fic]   81-19069
ISBN 0-201-15877-9   AACR2

To my two best friends,
Susan and Blythe

1

I'M twelve, almost thirteen, and I've got problems. Problems. Seems like that's the only thing people ever talk about anymore. School problems, skin problems, friend problems, and what-to-do-on-Friday-night problems. Well, why should I be any different?

My name is Boyd and I have two major problems. I have a lot more problems than just these two, but these are the most major.

The biggest problem right now is the fact that school starts in two weeks. I'm starting junior high. That shouldn't be that big of a deal, right? Wrong. I have to take P.E. sixth period and after P.E. I have to take a shower. The fact is I haven't hit puberty yet. In unscientific terms, I don't have hair yet.

You have to understand that everyone has hair except me. Everyone! We've got this guy in our class named Carl who has hair on his chest. He started shaving in the fourth grade. Is that fair? Here I am with a body that looks like the Sahara Desert, and King Kong Carl has enough hair for four people.

Okay, besides my puberty problems, my next biggest pain is the fact that I have two best friends. Wouldn't it be simple if my problem was that I just couldn't decide between two best friends? Too bad. That isn't the problem. The problem is my two best friends are girls.

We do everything together. We like most of the same things. We tell each other all our deep dark secrets. We are really truly best friends. Everyone in the world thinks it is weird for a thirteen-year-old boy to have two girls for best friends.

Now how would you like to have no pubic hairs and be faced with the horrible prospect of taking your clothes off in front of an entire P.E. class that thinks you're a weirdo because you have two girls for best friends? And I bet you thought you had problems because you've got a couple of zits.

This whole thing bothered me enough that I even thought of suicide. Marcia talked me out of it. She said suicide wasn't a viable option.

She says things like *viable option*. It drives people crazy. I kind of like it. Most of the time I can't believe that the words come out of her mouth. Once in sixth grade she got called on to answer some question. Marcia casually took off her glasses, which is a good sign that something big is going to come out of her mouth. She looked straight at stupid Mr. Franks and said, "Mr. Franks, you force me not only to ignore your insipid question but also to let you know that your motivational techniques to arouse my interest in this subject have failed miserably."

Wow! Mr. Franks wrote her a pass to the library. I looked up *insipid* in the dictionary. It means dull, a perfect word for Mr. Franks.

From that time on, I began reading the dictionary. I thought if a word like *insipid* could get you a pass to the library, just think what a word like *discombobulate* could do for you.

Marcia is pretty good at giving advice. She

ought to be. Her dad is a psychologist. My mother keeps calling him a psychiatrist. I keep telling her that he's a psychologist, which means he has a PhD in psychology. A psychiatrist is a medical doctor who specializes in psychiatry.

My mother said, "Since when did a sixth grader know so much about somebody who sits around and tells people to get divorces?"

I told her, "I know so much because Marcia tells me every time I turn around. Marcia also told me that he doesn't tell people to get divorces. She says he lets them decide. He never tells people what to do."

"What else does Marcia tell you?" Mother asked. But I knew she wasn't expecting an answer. It was her way of ending the conversation.

I think teachers are not only afraid of Marcia's ability to talk but are a little afraid of Marcia's dad. I'm a little afraid of him, too. There's something about him that makes me nervous. I'm always a little scared I'm going to say something dumb and he'll grab his beard, go hm–m–m, and then wrap a straitjacket around me. I confessed this to Marcia once and she told me that my ideas about mental illness and mental health came over on the *Mayflower.*

Marcia informed me, "Max"— she always calls her dad Max —"doesn't even work with the real crazies. He isn't into institutions or strait-jackets."

Her words of comfort didn't make it any easier for me to talk to Max. I thought it might be good for me to talk to him about my problems. Sort of work it into the conversation sometime when were alone. You ever try to work the subject of pubic hair into a conversation?

I mean you can't actually say, "How's your pubic hair, Max?"

He'd really think I was crazy.

WHEN I said I told Marcia and Lou everything, it wasn't the complete truth. I mean, I don't tell them all of everything. Although they are my best friends, they are girls, and as hard as I try, I can't quite tell them everything.

Like when I talked to Marcia about committing suicide I left out enough details so it wouldn't be embarrassing. I sort of told her I was generally depressed about growing up, stuff like that.

She said, "Depression is something I have some definite ideas about. I think we make way too big a deal about being depressed. I'm almost positive there'd be something wrong with you if you hit junior high and weren't depressed. At least you know at this stage you've got a chance to grow out of it."

Didn't I tell you she gave good advice?

About my other friend, Lou. Let's just say that Marcia and Lou are almost exact opposites. Whatever Marcia is, Lou isn't.

Marcia is, I guess, pretty. She's skinny, got long hair, sort of brown with these blonde streaks. "Remembrances of the summer" her mother calls them. Marcia says her mother writes sickening poetry. I can imagine.

Lou, on the other hand, is slightly overweight. Not fat, just overweight. She's also super-athletic. At one time she was going to be a lady wrestler. We talked her out of it. But every now and then she gets the urge and buys a wrestling magazine to, as she says, "just keep up on the field."

Lou has real short hair. Her hair is almost too short. No one else wears their hair that short but Lou doesn't seem to mind. Lou is her own person. She's also taken a couple of lessons in self-defense.

Which brings us to another fact about Lou. She takes tons of abuse. The fact is she's stronger than most boys her age. She can shoot free throws for an hour and never miss. She is also pretty good on the soccer field.

Most of the guys make fun of her. Marcia says they feel threatened. They call her Butch. Lou hates to be called Butch. That is why she took the self-defense classes.

She says, "Nobody calls me names and gets away with it. The first person that calls me Butch, I'm going to tear their face off."

I guess all you know about me is that I have problems and two pretty neat friends. Well, besides being grossly immature in the body department, I'm not too bad looking. Nothing great. I won't be a movie star or anything, but it wouldn't make you sick to look at me.

I've got overly long blonde hair that drives my dad berserk, and I've managed to wear the same pair of cutoffs all summer long with only washing them four times. That drives my mother crazy.

We're all three starting seventh grade this fall. Like I said the big day is in two weeks.

MOST of the time I try to forget how I met Lou. Her real name is Louella. Wouldn't you want to be called Lou?

When my mom and dad felt like they needed to make some changes in their lives, they decided we should move out of Los Angeles and picked Pine Springs to call home.

Dad took over as manager of the bank, and Mom unpacked her photography equipment and started taking pictures.

For me, moving here was a real shock. My parents had told me it would be a small town, but I had no idea that it would be *this* small! Pine Springs is so small that everybody knows everybody else. When you're new in town that can really make you feel left out. I felt the whole town was staring at me wherever I went.

Besides that, there was nothing to do. I mean, there were practically zero things to occupy your time. All I could think about, at first, was how I missed my old friends.

I hung around with a good gang in L.A. My best friend, Rod, promised he'd write a lot and let me know what everyone was up to. I got two long letters, one phone call, and from then on there was a postcard every so often. I must admit that by the time the postcards started to dribble in, I had some friends here and it was okay.

Now I didn't intentionally go out and try to make friends with a girl. It just happened. In L.A. nobody had girls for friends. You played with a cousin, maybe, if your parents made you, but you didn't make a habit out of it.

A week after we moved in, I knew that if I didn't make some new friends, I'd go berserk. Being an optimistic fourth-grader-going-into-fifth, I decided I might as well get it over with. So after breakfast I hopped onto my bike and went out to find a friend. You have to remember I was only a fourth-grader-going-into-fifth. Why else would I be dumb enough to think I was just going to ride around and make friends? I don't recall what I thought I'd use as an approach to meet people. I'm just thankful I wasn't so gooney that I went up to people and said, "Will you be my friend?"

Well, I rode my bike quite a while searching for friends and I was pretty discouraged, so I headed back to our new house which I hated. I'd seen a couple of kids but they were all way too young for me. When I got three blocks from my house, I saw this guy, about my height but a little heavier, lifting weights in his garage.

I put on my brakes and said real enthusiastically, "Hi!"

He said, "How's it going?"

That was all it took. I was in that garage talking a blue streak. I was telling this guy my most intimate secrets. I told him I had a copy of *Lady Chatterley's Lover* hidden under my mattress. Dumb stuff like that.

He just kept lifting weights, and I finally realized I'd told this guy everything about myself and I didn't even know his name. I thought for sure he'd pegged me for a first-class gooney.

He said, "Everyone calls me Lou."

I figured that Lou was a good name for someone who lifts weights as seriously as Lou did. I asked Lou some questions — stuff like how the school was here. I found out we were in the same grade. Pretty soon Lou asked me if I wanted to go swimming. I thought about it and said, "Sure."

Lou got his suit and we rode by my house to get mine and tell my mom where I was going. She was busy hanging her photographs. She's sure she's the next Margaret Bourke-White. She said something profound like, "That's nice. Don't drown." Everyone's a comedian.

With that we headed towards the pool. Since Pine Springs is so small, it doesn't take long to get to the pool no matter where you are starting from. Put that down as one of the plusses of Pine Springs.

We got to the pool, paid our money, and then, trying to act like I knew what I was doing, I followed Lou into the women's dressing room. That's right, folks. With eyes open I waltzed right into a room of screaming women.

In fact, you could hear the screams at least two blocks away. I ran out as fast as I could just as the lifeguard came running in, wanting to know what all the screaming was about.

She said real loud, "What's going on here?"

I heard Lou say, "Nothing."

Then the lifeguard said, "There had better not be," and walked out.

In the meantime, I'm in the hall very confused about what just happened. Lou finally stuck *his* head out of the door and said, "Stupid, the men's room is over there. I'll meet you outside."

I went in, got into my bathing suit, and walked out onto the deck of the pool. There was Lou in a girl's bathing suit, doing the best one-and-a-half I've ever seen.

Lou came over, laughing at me. I must have looked really shocked.

"You thought I was a boy. Didn't you?"

"Cripes, Lou," I said, "I sort of...I mean..."

She laughed really hard and started jumping around real crazy until everybody in the pool was looking at me.

The lifeguard said, "What is going on here?"

I'm sure that is the only line she learned at lifeguard school. I couldn't think of what to do, so when Lou settled down, I apologized. Lou told me that was stupid. She told me that she wasn't that hung up about being a girl and that it was an honest mistake.

"Don't be sorry. I'm not offended. Let's go meet Marcia. She's my best friend."

While we were swimming over to Marcia, she said, "Boyd, I think I'm going to like you. Your different from most of the creeps around here."

"Ya," I said, "I'm different all right. You must think I'm crazy or blind."

She said, "I can tell you're a little strange, but at least you're not afraid when you make a mistake to say you're sorry. Besides, I do look like a boy. Sometimes I like that and sometimes I don't. I think my dad doesn't mind, but my mother's a different story."

She stuck out her hand to shake mine and said, "Hey, let's be good friends, okay?"

"Sure," I said.

"You play basketball?" she asked.

"Ya," I answered.

"How good?"

I said, "Pretty good."

Lou asked, "How's your hook shot?"

"Lousy."

"I think we're going to get along fine," Lou said and smiled from ear to ear.

"Lou," I said, "would you teach me how to do a one-and-a-half?"

She said, "Sure. What are friends for anyway?"

I don't mind telling you that even the first time I met her, I thought Marcia was pretty neat. I liked the way she looked and talked and most everything about her.

From the time we started hanging around together, Marcia, Lou and I always had a good time. Both Marcia and Lou were different from anyone else I'd ever met, and they were so different from each other that we always kept ourselves amused.

I suppose I liked Marcia as more than just a friend right from the beginning, but we were having too much of a good time to make a big deal about it. Besides, I had enough problems. I wasn't ready for a romance.

I made some other friends besides Marcia and Lou. In fact, in about a month I got to know almost everyone in my class pretty well. After two months it seemed like Pine Springs wasn't going to be so bad after all. I didn't love it, but at least I liked it.

Even though I goofed around with the guys, I felt different about being with Marcia and Lou. I couldn't actually explain why I preferred their company. I just did.

I can look back now and see that although doing things with Marcia and Lou seemed to be more fun, there was also something else going on. Spending time with them was easier, somehow. It seemed more comfortable to talk to the two of them about things it would have been hard to talk to the guys about.

For instance, I couldn't say to John, who lived up the street and sat next to me in homeroom, "God, I feel suicidal." He wouldn't know what to say or do. Marcia, however, would begin a lengthy discussion, and Lou would tell me to stop eating sugar and go running.

With the guys it seemed like we could only do certain activities and talk about things like sports or sound systems. We mostly teased each other or joked around rather than saying what we really felt.

I know people thought it was strange that I hung around Marcia and Lou and that we were all just good friends, but with both of them I felt more like myself. I could relax. I never had to worry about doing or saying the right thing to make sure they would like me.

My folks had adjusted to moving here fairly well. My mother kept saying she was having culture withdrawal. She often said she would consider selling her soul for a walk through a decent art gallery. But she made some friends and found lots of new places to photograph.

My father loved everything about living in Pine Springs. He constantly reminded us that he was doing things here he'd meant to do his whole life. He especially worked in the yard a lot. He grew tomatoes but they never seemed to produce anything but blossoms. He said the fun was in the growing.

He also mowed the lawn more times than anyone else in town. Whenever he was bored, in a bad mood, or even in a good mood, he'd mow the lawn. One weekend he tried his hand at building lawn furniture. He built a picnic table. It collapsed to the ground the first time we tried to eat on it. He said the fun was in the building.

Both Lou and Marcia like my folks and my folks like them. My mom thought it was good for me to have some girls as friends. ("There will be other women in your life, Boyd, and you'll have to know how to relate to them," she told me.) Dad seemed to think it was okay as long as I also had boys as friends.

I particularly like Marcia's folks even though her dad makes me nervous. They always treat us with a lot of respect and lots of good food.

I am not exactly crazy about Lou's parents. (Neither is she.) They are something else. Her dad is a retired Air Force Captain who would rather have had a boy as his only child instead of a girl (even if she is nicknamed Lou). Sometimes he treats me like a new recruit ("Stand tall, Boyd, my boy!") and sometimes like a nephew or something.

Lou's dad likes to watch us play games to make sure we are good enough competition to, as he says, "keep Louella on her toes." Competition is a super-big thing with him.

Lou's mom is hearty, like her husband, but Lou says her mother would prefer it if Lou acted more "like a lady." She tries to get Lou interested in "quiet" activities like sewing and découpage. Lou can do that kind of thing, but she's a whole lot happier on a court or field or in a pool—not just sitting around.

Lou says her mother has mostly given up on getting her to act like a little princess. Every now and then, however, she gets disgusted with the way Lou looks and acts, and she goes on a campaign to change her. Lou says her mom tries to fix her up—her clothes, her hair, her hobbies—and then gives up.

Once when she was in that fix-up mood, Lou's mom asked Lou to bake a cake. Lou doesn't mind cooking at all so it was no big deal. However, she also knew her mother was on one of her campaigns.

Lou baked the cake. She told her mother it was junk food but for her she'd do it. It was a chocolate cake, and when it came time to frost it, Lou used brown and green frosting and decorated it like a muddy football field after a game in a rainstorm.

Her mother hasn't asked her to bake a cake since.

SCHOOL starts in two weeks.
If I didn't know it for a fact
from reading it in the paper
or from someone constantly
reminding me, I'd know it from
the smell. You can smell school
creeping up on you a mile away.

It starts with just a little
tinge of something in the air.
It's what people, like my dad,
usually call "the hint of fall in
the air" or "the whisper of

approaching autumn." Well it isn't a hint or whisper of anything. It is school slapping you in the face.

You know how it smells. Like fresh lavatory deodorizers newly removed from their packages. It smells like school cooking. It smells like big pots of gooey macaroni. The worst is the smell of those clean floors. That smell is enough to kill you. I get depressed even thinking about it.

How do those smells get out and fill the whole area at just the right time? It's a plot of some kind. It's a form of chemical warfare working on our nasal passages. I explained this theory to Marcia.

Marcia's reply was, "My dad has an empty slot in his appointment schedule for this afternoon."

Lou knows what I mean. She says she smells it, too. The difference is—she likes the smell. To her it smells like a clean locker room ready to be filled with sweaty bodies.

Which brings me to another point about Lou. She is turning out for the boys' soccer team this year. She calls it the "persons' soccer team." I was still up in the air about whether or not I wanted to join the team but Lou was more than hopeful.

"Are you going to turn out and help us become state champions?" asked Lou as we sat on my front porch, eating roasted soybeans. We were eating soybeans because Lou does not believe in any form of junk food.

"They don't have state championships for junior high soccer," I replied.

"That's beside the point."

"What is the point then?" I asked.

"Well, are you going to be on the team with me or not? I'm going to need you."

I hadn't thought of it but if Lou was going to survive the verbal abuse she was going to get on the team, she was going to need a friend there to support her. Who was I to refuse a friend in need?

"Sure. Okay. I'll turn out."

"All right! Well then, you have to get your physical right away. The results have to be at the school and approved by this Friday."

I told her I hated doctors but she didn't listen. She walked past me and charged into my house. She told my mother I was turning out for soccer and asked her to call and make an appointment for me to get a physical by Friday.

"Lou," I said, "I'm not sure I really want to play soccer and I'm sure I don't want a physical. Do they draw blood?"

"Not much," comforted Lou.

"Besides, I'm awful at soccer. You've said so yourself."

Lou started to look real hurt so I tried to convince myself I could use the exercise. I even tried to act enthusiastic, but all I could think about was the doctor's office and a possible blood test.

After a significant pause I said, "Okay."

My mother called the doctor while Lou outlined for me how we were going to get in shape. I pictured the doctor, like some vampire, sucking me dry of blood. Suddenly I remembered. You have to remove your clothes in a physical. Great! Not only am I going to lose my blood but this doctor, who has probably seen everyone else's body in my class, is going to see how immature mine is. Will he recommend hormones?

My mother got off the phone. "They can work you in right now if you hurry on over to the clinic."

All I could say was, "But . . . " and "Isn't it a little fast?"

"C'mon," shouted Lou as she pushed me out the door. "You could be the next Pelé."

I didn't want to be the next Pelé but that was beside the point. Lou had us running all the way downtown to start getting in shape. I had another terrifying thought. I couldn't remember if I had clean underwear on or not.

We were halfway there when we passed Marcia. She was talking to a jerk. Jack, what a jerk. He's two years older than we are and does he ever think he's something. Well, he's something all right. He's a jerk.

We had barely passed her when Marcia realized it was us. She hollered at us to wait up. We yelled back that we couldn't because we were in a hurry.

She and Jack started running after us and Marcia yelled, "Where are you going?"

I knew it was a mistake but we slowed down, letting them almost catch up with us.

"To the doctor's office," I replied.

Before Marcia could ask why, Lou volunteered that we were both turning out for soccer and I had to get a physical. That was all it took.

Jack the Jerk started laughing. "That's all our soccer team needs—a girl and a nerd."

At that moment, just as he pronounced nerd, I fell. Yes, I tripped and fell. Jack came close to choking he was laughing so hard. I ground gravel into the palms of my hands. I now had a real reason to go to the doctor.

Lou picked me up. "Stick it. You're not so

hot," she told Jack. I didn't say a word. We continued on to the doctor's office. My hands were bleeding and Lou was breathing down my neck to get me to hurry up. I knew falling was an omen of what was to come. I believe in omens. Why didn't I turn around and go home?

WE walked into the doctor's office. I managed to spit out that my mother had just called and they had said I could get right in.

The nurse said, "Huh?"

Another omen. I wondered how many omens you need to discover you are on the wrong track?

Look at Oedipus. He was this king that Marcia made me read about . She says the Oedipus complex is something I should know about. It's a pretty good story even though someone told me I should read it.

In a real short version, this king, Oedipus, kills his father and marries his own mother. Everyone had omens that the whole thing would happen but they couldn't stop him from killing his dad and marrying his mom. The problem was, Oedipus didn't know it was his dad that he killed and he didn't know it was his mom that he married. Anyway, in the end he realizes what he's done and goes nuts and pokes his eyes out.

That doesn't have much to do with being at the doctor's office but it has a lot to do with ignoring omens.

The nurse looked in her book and said, "Yes, we're going to fit you in. Soccer, huh? Here take this in there and when you are done bring it back to me."

She handed me this jar that looked like something we use in science lab. We both looked at it a second, and then she said, "A specimen, we need a specimen."

Honest to God, I had no idea what she was talking about, and of all the dumb things to do, I said, "I don't understand."

She looked around the room like she was trying to get everybody's attention so they won't miss a word and then yelled—well, said—a whole lot louder than was necessary, "A urine specimen."

She pronounced it real slow. It sounded like it should have echoed. If you spelled it out the way it sounded, it would probably look like this: U—U—R—R—I—I—N—N—E. Now I ask you, how could you trust someone with your life when they couldn't even talk right? Lou was hiding behind a *National Geographic* shaking the building with her laughing.

I took the bottle and went into the rest room. What if I couldn't go? What if I overflowed? Couldn't stop? I managed to control my fears and got the specimen okay. My next step was to nonchalantly walk out and hand it to the nurse.

I covered up the bottle with my hand so you couldn't see it. It felt really strange to be holding a bottle of urine.

I opened the door and tried to act like it was no big deal. I was acting like I did this every day. Remember the trouble that kind of thinking got me into at the swimming pool?

I stepped out into the hall just in time to hit a blur of white coming around the corner. You won't believe it. The omens were right. I wanted to poke both my eyes out. There was the nurse with my urine down the front of her uniform.

I thought she'd puke on the spot, but she didn't. I sure would've if I'd been her, but I suppose nurses are trained to handle things like that. Well, she might not have puked, but she sure gave me a dirty look.

The doctor came out of a room, took one look at the nurse, and turned around and went back in. Another nurse came over with a new bottle. She was laughing so super-hard and trying not to do it out loud that her shoulders shook.

"Here," she said, "try to keep it in the bottle this time."

Was I ever embarrassed. What was worse, here I was standing in the rest room again, trying to urinate when I had just gone ten seconds ago.

Afterwards, I sat on a table in a small room reading a five-year-old *Sports Illustrated*. When the doctor finally came in he said, "Drop your pants and turn and cough."

So I took off my pants. Luckily I did have clean underwear. I then proceeded to turn completely around, back to where I started from, and coughed. The doctor started laughing. I thought for sure he was laughing at my grossly immature body.

But then he said, "I'm sorry. I meant to say, 'turn your head and cough.' "

"Oh," I said, turning my head.

He finished the hernia test. I knew it was the hernia test because he marked it off on the exam sheet. I almost asked him for a shot of hormones but what would he say? If something was wrong, wouldn't he tell me?

He told me I could get dressed so I mumbled something about being sorry for the accident with the nurse. He'd seemed to have forgotton the whole thing, but when I left the room and shut the door, I heard the distinct sound of uncontrolled laughter. Was he laughing at my body? Or was he laughing at the nurse?

Lou saw me come out and yelled, "Did you throw up on anybody?"

I surprised myself and managed to yell back, "Real funny, Butch."

"What'd you call me?"

"Butch," I said weakly.

"Could I have your hand, please?"

"What for?"

"Just give me your hand."

You remember I told you how Lou had learned self-defense so she could clobber the next person that called her Butch? How could I forget that?

I gave her my hand and the next thing I knew I was lying flat on my back on the waiting room floor. I opened my eyes and there was my favorite nurse in a clean uniform, grinning at me from ear to ear.

She said one thing, "It serves you right."

I felt depressed. What did she
mean, "It serves me right?"
As if I'm to blame. I didn't
ask to turn out for soccer. I
didn't ask to get a physical.
For that matter, I didn't ask
to be born.

The only thing to do when I
felt depressed was to go talk
to Marcia. Some people have the
knack for getting you out of a
bad mood. Marcia's got the knack.

I went over to Marcia's. She was at home but so was Max.

"Max is with a client. We'll have to go into my room."

Now that's another thing about growing up. A year ago it was no big deal that I was in a girl's bedroom. Now that I'm going into seventh grade suddenly everybody, mainly my parents, raises their eyebrows so high they look like they've just got a new face-lift whenever you mention the word bedroom.

I want to say, "I know what you are thinking and I don't even have pubic hair yet. So forget it!"

Marcia has a neat room. She fills it with all sorts of junk. It gets pretty cluttered-looking but that's part of what makes it neat.

She's a collector. Her room is filled with antique bottles, old photographs, a huge collection of miniature doll furniture, a collection of glass animals, thousands of records (mostly classical), and books everywhere.

"What are these?" I asked as I moved a pile of books to sit down.

"Books last time I looked."

"Everyone's a comedian. I know they're books but what are they for?"

"They were my summer reading project."

The reason I asked was because I never had seen such a pile of thick, thick books in my life. I looked at the titles. There was *Moby Dick, The Complete Works of Shakespeare,* and *Pilgrim's Progress,* among others.

"Yuck," I said, "did you read any of them?"

"Just the good parts."

I took a quick look through *Moby Dick.* "It's overdue. What are you keeping these around for anyway?"

"I like the way they look. I think they sort of fit the room. What do you think?"

How are you supposed to answer a question like that?

I said, "Yes."

Marcia got things around to the business at hand.

"Why did you let Lou talk you into playing soccer? You told me you hated soccer."

When she gets to the point she really gets to the point. I told her that I felt Lou needed me on the team to give her support. I also said I could use the exercise.

"Lou doesn't need anyone. She's strong, and when she knows what she wants, she gets it."

"But she wanted me to, " I said.

"So. It is still your decision. All I'm trying to say is you can't blame Lou. It's your choice whether to turn out or not."

"Okay, cut the therapy. I'm turning out because I want to. I'm also turning out because I want to support Lou."

"Just don't mope around about it."

"Maybe I better go," I said.

"If you want to."

"How come you're so cranky?"

"What did you want me to say?"

I wanted her to say how sorry she felt for me, how wonderful I was for sacrificing myself this way. Well, wasn't I?

Deep down, I knew she was right. Lou didn't need me in that way. She could use a little support, but she'd still make it on her own. If I was turning out for soccer, I had to do it for myself.

"I'll have to think about it," I told Marcia. We arranged to walk to school together the first day of classes. When I got home, I went in to my room and stretched out across the bed.

I made a list of reasons why turning out for soccer would be good or bad. I came up with four reasons why I should turn out:

1. I'd get in shape.

2. It would give me something to do after school.

3. I could help Lou.

4. I might be a professional soccer player someday.

I could think of only one reason why I shouldn't do it:

1. I wasn't sure I was any good at it.

I definitely had more reasons why I should turn out than why I shouldn't. It was decided. I'd go ahead and turn out for soccer. I went outside and practiced bouncing the ball off my head. Maybe I *would be* the next Pelé.

I remembered I hadn't told Marcia about the nurse. I called her up. She split a gut.

T HE next week before school
started, before soccer turnout
started, we practiced like crazy.
We meaning Lou and me. Marcia
would occasionally join in
but she always let us know that
"competitive sports are completely
overemphasized in this country
and I'm only doing this to keep
in shape."

Marcia always joined us
for our 6:00 A.M. run. The

run was something Lou thought up. Somehow running is supposed to be better for you if you're half asleep. Once you get going it isn't so bad, but getting going is something else. I couldn't believe the things that were up and moving at that time. They even looked happy.

The only reason I ever considered doing the run was that everyday Marcia invited us to breakfast at her house afterward. It was fantastic. Marcia's mom, and once Max, made wonderful breakfasts. They were the kind of breakfasts you see in magazines. Stuff like omelets and waffles with strawberries. Real fancy stuff. Marcia said that breakfast was a meal her mother enjoyed cooking. My mother neither enjoys cooking nor breakfast.

We'd spend a couple of hours eating breakfast and sipping iced tea on their deck, and then Lou and I would head on up to the school activity field for some dribbling practice.

I remember when I was in grade school we had a P.E. teacher who did nothing but make us practice dribbling. If it wasn't a soccer ball, it was a basketball. Every day he'd say, "How about some dribbling practice?"

And every day we'd look at him and let the saliva drool over our lips so we were dribbling.

Get it? What a bunch of jerks. I don't think that coach ever caught on. That is one thing I've noticed; coaches aren't too swift in the joke department.

I've made a mental note not to try any jokes on Mr. Sandwich, our soccer coach. He looks like he doesn't joke around much. He also looks like he eats a loaf of Wonder bread at every meal.

I'm not so hot at dribbling. Dribbling in soccer, that is. I'm pretty good with a basketball. In soccer you have to move and control the ball with your feet, without falling over it. Not falling over the ball is very important. It is also something, with my recent history of coordination, that I'm working hard at improving.

We'd dribble around the field awhile. Then we'd practice a few kicks and stuff. I'm better at that. Then we'd go over to Lou's to hoist a little iron. However, we didn't usually hoist too much. We'd end up reading comic books, eating some lunch, and then getting Marcia and heading for the swimming pool.

The one thing I miss most when school starts is the swimming pool. They close it the first day of school. It's totally unfair. It's like going cold turkey off summer. The least they could do is leave it open a little longer so you could sort of ease off one and into the other.

Let's say they let you start going to school only a couple of hours each day, letting you swim and goof around the rest of the time. They could slowly work up to a full day of school. By then it would be too cold to swim so it would be okay. Sounds like a perfect idea to me. Remind me to bring it up with the school board.

Maybe if they had a swimming pool at the school, it would be easier to start in the fall. On second thought, I doubt it. They'd find a way to make it boring. They'd for sure make us line up and swim in straight lines. That's loads of fun. If anyone or anything can make something boring, school can.

We spent our last five days of freedom working out and hanging out. In that short time I didn't improve my soccer much, but I gained a little confidence. I knew I'd never be great, but I thought I could definitely make some improvements. I wanted to be an okay player who wasn't an embarassment to the team. It seemed like a reasonable goal.

Now if I could only figure out how to either grow hair or take a shower with my clothes on, I'd be all set.

I yelled through Lou's back door, "Hurry up or we'll be late."

"What's your hurry?" she answered.

Then I fainted. Lou came outside wearing a dress. I didn't really faint but I could have. Lou looked ridiculous.

She took one look at my expression and walked back into the house, slamming the screen door.

"That does it. I'm not walking around having everyone stare at me like I'm some kind of freak."

In less than five minutes she was back outside wearing jeans and a T-shirt.

"You're right," I said. "That thing—that dress—wasn't really you."

"You were right the first time. That *was* a thing. Something my mother would wear. You know what I felt like dressed like that? Ridiculous!"

Lou was all red in the face and I could tell she'd probably fought with her mother for hours, maybe days, about it. I guess I'm lucky. I have to fight about getting my hair cut, but at least clothes aren't such a big thing.

"She can't accept me for what I am. No one can."

"Hey, that isn't true. I do, Lou."

"Really? Do you think I'm okay or do you think I'm some overweight freak who should get a sex change?"

"Jeez, Lou, if I didn't think you were okay, do you think I'd spend my time with you?"

"Boyd, can I ask you a personal question?"

"Sure."

"Do you think of me as a girl or as one of the guys?"

"I think of you as Lou. Why'd you ask that?"

"Because my mother said, if I don't start acting like a lady, I'm always going to be one of the guys."

"Swear to God, I think of you as Lou, my friend."

Okay, so I said the right thing. Lou looked at me and smiled. She then turned to her house and yelled, "Maybe I want to be one of the guys. Did you ever think of that?"

We walked toward Marcia's without saying anything.

"Hey, thanks," she said, "I feel better now. In fact, I feel so good that I'll race you to Marcia's house."

Marcia was ready and sitting out on the front steps.

"What gives? How come you're out here waiting?"

I was surprised. Marcia isn't the type to be eager to get to school.

"I guess I got used to getting up early, and besides I've decided to change my attitude about school. I'm going to try to be interested in the boring crap they'll attempt to cram down our throats."

"You won't make it," Lou told her.

"I know," said Marcia, "but it's worth a try, isn't it? Besides I promised Max I wouldn't be so critical. He's convinced my attitude makes me miss the good stuff they have to offer when it comes around."

"If it comes around," I added.

We all said at once, "If."

Off we went, seekers of truth or knowledge, whichever comes first. Junior high—look out! And who should be waiting at the front door of school? None other than Jack himself.

He said, "Hey, Marcia, can I talk to you a second?" He paused for a second just looking at us. He then added, "Alone?"

"What does he want?" said Lou.

We were soon to find out because Marcia went over and talked to him. He sure looked nervous. It wasn't two minutes before she was back with us.

"You'll never believe what that was all about."

We didn't. Jack the Jerk had asked Marcia to the dance Saturday night.

"Well, are you going?" asked Lou.

"Yes, but not with Jack."

"Who are you going with?" I asked. The minute I said it I freaked because I knew my voice sounded funny.

"I told him I had a date with you two. I also told him I'd dance with him once we were there."

"What did he say?" asked Lou.

"He said he'd see me there. It was no big thing. Really."

"No big thing?" screamed Lou. "You just got asked on a date for the first time and it is no big deal? My mother would die if I got asked on a date. She'd have a heart attack from sheer joy."

"Lou, are you living in the Dark Ages?" Marcia answered back.

They both looked at me, waiting for me to say something. I was completely shocked that Marcia didn't say yes to him. I couldn't think of anything to say.

Finally Lou said, "So we're all three going together. Good. That'll give them something to talk about."

"You're coming with us, aren't you?" Marcia said looking straight into my eyes.

"Well, yes—of course," I managed to spit out, "but I didn't even know there was a dance."

"Talk about living in the Dark Ages," said Lou.

It seems that every year there is a junior high dance honoring the new students which means us, the seventh graders. Its one of the school traditions.

Now here I was going on my first date with not one but two girls. Lou was right. It would certainly give them something to talk about.

The bell rang. We walked through the doors and pushed our way through the thick smell of macaroni and cheese. Homeroom, what a joke. Nothing homey about it. Oh, well, school had begun.

10

THE whole day was insane. The teachers tried to fill whole periods with passing out books. Passing out books takes about fifteen minutes if you really stretch it out. So for the rest of the time the kids took over and accomplished a few things.

To keep the count straight there were:

- Four spit-wad fights.
- One food fight (lunch).
- Three kids kicked out of class.
- One teacher who threatened to kill us before the year was over.
- Two teachers who promised to kill us before the day was over.

Some unusual records set during the day included:

- Tom smoking twenty cigarettes.
- Tom throwing up from smoking twenty cigarettes.
- Lynette asking to go to the rest room thirty-eight times. She got to go eight times.
- Dave sleeping through four out of six classes.
- Marcia managing to get sent to the library three times.

I wonder why she just doesn't report there in the morning.

Sixth period was okay. It was P.E. It came and went real fast. Most of the guys hadn't brought their gym clothes so we didn't have to undress or suit-up.

Mr. Sandwich went on and on about keeping

fit. I think he should try it himself sometime. He then let everyone who wasn't turning out for soccer go to the library.

His last words were, "Everybody be here tommorrow with your clothes and that means your own jockstrap not your brother's."

Jack the Jerk said, "How about your sister's?" The seventh and eighth graders were all in the same P.E. class.

Everyone started laughing. I don't know why, but I was laughing, too. Okay, so it was a little funny, but I was laughing my fool head off. It wasn't that funny. If I had been in any other situation, I might have laughed a little, but I sure wouldn't have gotten hysterical.

Now this is something I'm not sure I quite understand. It's like you walk into a locker room and you become someone else. You smell the sweat and instantly you turn into the Incredible Hulk. Everyone talks differently than they do any other time of the day.

Like I said, I don't get it. I can't see how I can be one person in fifth period and another person in sixth period. But I was doing it. I was being "one of the guys" and laughing at Jack's dumb joke.

The period ended and I started suiting-up for soccer practice. It was okay because I kind of turned my back to most of the guys and undressed and dressed real fast. Three or four guys were standing around talking about sex.

It was a little strange listening to them. It's almost as if because they were in a locker room, they were expected to talk about sex. So they did. They made it sound like going to the toilet in a dirty rest room. Get what I mean?

I never mind when Marcia and Lou and I talk about it. Actually, I mind a little. I mean they *are* girls and I'm a boy, but it's not as embarassing as you might think, especially if we don't talk about very specific details. Marcia sort of leads the discussion because she tends to know the most.

She says,"Max says that most people hate their bodies. That is the reason that they talk about sex in a dirty way."

She says that we should talk about sex as a choice. You know, like making a decision about it rather than just letting it happen. We talk a lot about taking care of yourself, not letting someone use you.

I worry a little, maybe more than a little,

that I hate my body. I know I don't like it. I wish it were more mature. I'm not sure if that's hate or not.

Those guys talking about sex in the locker room—I wondered if they hated their bodies. They probably do. If you took a poll of kids in junior high, I bet most of them would say they don't like their bodies.

Soon I was out on the field running two miles, which is Mr. Sandwich's idea of a warm-up. Warming up is one thing. Dying of the heat is another. I was running and thinking about Marcia. I felt different about her ever since this morning when Jack asked her to the dance.

Suddenly I'm thinking about Marcia in a different way, and the idea of Marcia and Jack going to the dance makes me feel kind of jealous. It's as if somebody threw a bucket of cold water over me. I should have known right then and there that I was starting to like Marcia as more than a friend. In fact, I was falling in love.

Then I started thinking about Lou. What would it do to Lou if Marcia and I were more than friends? You've heard the old saying, "Three's a crowd." What would happen to our happy-go-lucky group?

Just then Jack came running up behind me. "Hey, what's with you and those two girls?"

"We're just good friends," I said.

"Well, it looks funny to me, you hanging around them all the time. You funny or something?"

"What is that supposed to mean?" I asked, sounding tougher than I wanted to.

"Well, kid, it means are you funny?"

That's all he said as he ran ahead of me. I knew he was just mad because Marcia wouldn't go to the dance with him. I knew he was trying to get even with me. But it still bugged me that he called me funny.

Lou. Good old Lou. She came up behind me and slugged me so hard that I tripped on the side of the track, fell down, and almost knocked the wind out of myself.

Mr. Sandwich yelled across the field, "On your feet, Boyd. You can't play soccer lying down."

"I'm sorry," Lou said weakly.

Sometimes I really feel like hauling off and hitting her one. That girl doesn't know her own strength.

Jack came running up behind us.

"Well, what do we have here? A funny guy on the ground and a Butch who put him there."

"Cram it, Jack, or I'll break your arm," Lou said for both of us. The whistle blew. We ran over to Coach Sandwich who promised to make soccer players out of us even if it killed us. I told you he has no sense of humor at all.

11

THE second day of school was a little better. We held class elections in each homeroom. Besides having student-body officers, every class has a president, vice president, and a combination secretary and treasurer. Nobody wants to be the secretary-treasurer.

Our whole seventh-grade class consists of only thirty-three kids. "We're small potatoes," Lou always says. So the elections are no big thing unless someone nominates you for an office. Then it's pretty embarrassing to have the whole class voting for or against you. What's bad is if you lose, and it's even worse if you lose by a huge margin, like when your opponent gets all the votes and the person who nominated you doesn't even vote for you.

I thought I was pretty safe. I figured I wasn't the class-officer type. Marcia says that school elections are nothing but popularity contests, and I wouldn't exactly give myself the Most Popular Person Award in my class. I walked into homeroom pretty secure that I would sit there and read a book. I turned out to be totally wrong.

I sat down, listened to the bell ring, and started talking to John while Ms. Lexington took attendance. When she finished she told us to be quiet and started the class meeting. She explained that we would elect a president right off so that he or she could continue the meeting.

At this point Lou shot out of her seat and said, "I nominate Boyd for president and move that nominations be closed, or whatever it is that you do to get down to voting."

I could have killed her.

Ms. Lexington told Lou her nomination was

fine and that *closed* was the right word but maybe we should have at least one more candidate. She asked, "Do we have any more nominations?"

Someone in the back yelled, "Marcia." I couldn't believe it. Everyone knew we were friends.

Lou and Marcia exchanged glances, and I thought I saw Marcia nod to Lou, as if to say, "It's okay. I don't mind and Boyd won't mind either."

Ms. Lexington said, "All right, may we have campaign speeches from the two candidates? Marcia, would you go first please?"

Marcia went to the front of the room to give her speech, and I sat at my desk with the absolute certainty that within thirty seconds I was going to throw up—or worse. I can't make speeches.

I really can't speak in front of large groups. Whenever I try, nothing comes out. I end up coughing, then saying the first thing that comes to mind. That first thing is always pretty *inane*.

Marcia looked as calm as ever. She smiled at me and then started her speech like it was something she did every day.

"Friends, Romans, classmates, lend me

your ears," she started. She might have ended right there. I heard Lou groan, and John said, "I'm not Roman; I'm Protestant."

Marcia continued like she didn't even notice. She covered human rights, the nature of creativity, the theory of relativity, her views on foreign policy, made a reference to the Spanish Inquisition, and ended, of course, with Sigmund Freud.

"The great question Freud was unable to answer, despite years of research into the feminine soul, is 'What does a woman want?' I would just like to say that what this woman wants is to be president of this class. Thank you."

I sat there with my mouth open. Lou clapped wildly and said, "You tell 'em, Marcia." A couple of girls in the front row clapped, but most of the kids snickered or looked confused.

Before I could figure out whose side Lou really was on, John said to me, "If you get up to the front of the room and don't fall down, I think you've won."

Ms. Lexington said, "Boyd, would you like to make a speech?"

I said, "No," and the whole class broke up.

I walked to the front of the class. I coughed like I knew I would. Then I opened my mouth and said, "I just want to say, uh, well, I think that if I become president of this class, I'll try to, uh, well, I'll try to make sure we get more dances and uh, well, I'd like to say, uh, I'd like to be the class president. Thank you."

As I went, blushing, to my seat, I saw Lou jump up and burst into applause. I glanced around and saw the rest of the class clapping also.

Ms. Lexington said, "Marcia and Boyd, please step out into the hall so we can tally the votes."

Out in the hall, Marcia and I laughed at how stupid the whole thing was and then we looked at each other not knowing what to say. Marcia finally said, "Well, I guess you'll probably win."

"Forget it," I answered, but I hoped she was right.

"Why do I do it?" Marcia said. "When will I learn not to show off like that? It's as if I don't want people to like me."

"It wasn't that bad," I said. "In fact, I was impressed." We looked at each other.

"Well, it's no big deal," Marcia said. "Whoever loses will become vice president, so it's not like losing completely."

"I think Lou has completely lost her mind,"

I said. "First she nominates me, then she cheers you, then she claps for me."

"She couldn't really take sides, could she? Anyway, Lou knows either one of us will be a great class president."

"Well, good luck," I sighed.

"If you say, 'May the best man win,' I'll scream." Then she added, "I'll still love you whether you win or not."

I almost choked. No female had ever said she loved me except my mother. The trouble was I didn't know if Marcia meant it like she was one of the family or if she really meant it.

"You will?" I asked and my voice cracked.

Just then the door opened and the whole class cheered as Ms. Lexington told me I was class president and Marcia was vice president. Marcia laughed and yelled, "Blatant sexism." No one else laughed because most of them, once again, had no idea what Marcia was talking about.

I went up to the front to run the rest of the meeting. Marcia didn't act hurt or anything. She was busy making jokes and actually cracking up the entire class. She moved that we have an ambassador to the moon to be sent on an interplanetary mission at once. She quickly nominated Mr. Shed, our principal.

Before Ms. Lexington knew what was happening, we had closed the nominations and voted him in. Everyone seemed to be having a good time. I wasn't feeling any pain, but looking over at Marcia, I had to admit I admired her cool. I couldn't help wondering how I would have felt and acted if I had been the one who'd lost.

When the meeting was over, Lou came up and slapped me on the back and said, "Congratulations."

"Oh," I said, forgetting my previous vow to kill her, "it was nothing."

As I started to leave, Lou stuck out her foot and tripped me. "Just wanted to make sure you weren't getting conceited," she said, smiling sweetly. Marcia, who had been right behind her, looked at Lou, and they laughed as if it was the funniest thing that had ever happened.

"Hey," I said, rubbing my shin, "are you two ganging up on me? Remember, Lou, you nominated me in the first place."

"But you'll never know who I actually voted for," Lou said, winking at Marcia.

I must have looked puzzled because Marcia and Lou each put an arm around me. "Listen," Lou said, "I'm just proud to know that my two good friends are class leaders."

"Onwards and upwards," Marcia said, giving me a little hug.

I wasn't feeling any pain at all.

12

THE rest of the week was pretty much the same. Nuts! The only thing that saved the week was that everyone was pretty excited about the dance Saturday night. It was also announced that we would have a practice game against Rosehedge on Saturday morning.

It was Thursday at practice that Coach Sandwich announced who would start in the practice game. He gave a long speech on how he picks the players that work the hardest during the week to start in the games.

The shock came when I found out that both Lou and I were starting. I wasn't surprised for Lou but I didn't think I would make it. I guess the early morning runs had paid off. On second thought maybe I got lucky.

Jack the Jerk was picked, too. He wasn't too happy that Lou and I were. He hadn't let up all week. He'd been calling me names, tripping me, stuff like that. I'd been ignoring him because I didn't know what else to do.

After the announcement Coach Sandwich told us to run a mile to warm up. We all groaned real heavy so he made it a mile and a half. I tell you this guy is a laugh a minute.

Lou and I started out at a trot and pretty soon Jack was alongside us giving us his typical crap.

"Who's going to ask who to dance among you three this Saturday night?"

"Get lost, Jack. If I want to dance, I can ask someone," answered Lou.

"Is that right? Well, before you ask me to dance let's see how fast you are on your feet."

With that Jack the Jerk tripped Lou while giving the upper part of her body a shove. The action sent her sprawling on the track.

"That does it," I said, sounding a bit like Superman.

I hauled off and slugged him in the gut. I managed to knock the wind out of him in the process. Needless to say, I was pretty proud of myself.

Lou got up. She was real mad and the thing that gets me is that she was almost as mad at me as she was at Jack.

"I don't need anyone to protect me or defend me. You understand?"

"I was just trying to help," I said.

"Well, don't," was Lou's reply.

She reached down and offered her hand to Jack who was sitting on the ground catching his breath. What an idiot. He took her hand, she helped him up, and then she flipped him and left him lying on his back.

"You three get in here. I want to talk to you," yelled Coach Sandwich.

All I could think about were all the names Jack had called me, that Lou was mad at me, and I was probably being kicked off the team. We went into the coach's office. Jack was still having trouble breathing and said he had a headache. I assured him that the headache was from the flip and would go away at least in a week.

"Why'd you hit me?" he asked me.

"Because you tripped Lou. That's why."

"I didn't think you had it in you. I didn't think you were man enough."

Coach Sandwich interrupted our conversation with a long lecture on team spirit and mutual support ending with, "If you ever pull this kind of crap again, or if I even hear of you three not being the very ideal of friendship, you're off the team."

Lou asked if we were still going to start.

"I'll have to think about it," he said. "We'll see how much you hustle out there today."

What did Jack think I had in me? I felt like the same old Boyd. But just because I slugged him in the gut, Jack now saw me as a completely new person. A man. You hit somebody and you're a man. I must have peaked early because physically I'm barely there. I don't even have hair in the right places.

13

THE next day, Friday, was the day before the practice game and also the day before the dance. Everyone was totally wired. Marcia got up in science quoting William Blake about seeing the world in a grain of sand. She blew everyone away including the teacher and, of course, got a pass to the library.

I passed Jack in the hall several times but he didn't say anything. No names, nothing.

Marcia, Lou and I sat out on the grass in the smokers' park across from school to eat lunch. We call it that because that's where all the dope smokers go to get themselves ready for school. We may act like dopes sometimes but we don't smoke it.

We were into peanut butter, and it seemed like the air was pretty clear of smoke for a change.

"I've had it," Marcia said. "I'm not even going to make it through eighth grade so I can legally quit. If I spend one more minute in the library I'm going to die."

Lou said, "Well, if you wouldn't say those weird things, you could stay in class with the rest of us."

"Great," Marcia shot back, "so I can die of boredom in there."

"What's wrong with the library," I asked. "At least you can do what you want."

"What I want is to get out of here!"

"What would you do?" asked Lou.

"I don't know. Why do I have to do anything? School is ludicrous. I should stay at home. I should go to Europe. I should go to work."

Lou said, "You should turn out for soccer."

I reminded Marcia she "shouldn't" do anything. She gave me a look that could kill and then continued on.

"I'm in seventh grade and I feel like I'm wasting my life away. It all seems so stupid and pointless. I'm going to school because of some law."

"You're in the gifted program," said Lou. "What do you want?"

"I don't know! Sometimes I want to stay home but then I'd miss you guys. I want to feel like I'm really doing something, something great. Instead, I feel like if you aren't into the dance Saturday night or dope or soccer you've got nothing. Don't you see, we're bored out of our minds!"

"I'm not bored," said Lou.

I said, "But you've got different goals, and I'm not just thinking of soccer." Marcia almost smiled at my pun. "Seriously, though, soccer is something really worth doing for you, Lou."

"I understand what you're talking about," Lou said, "but I figure if you can't beat 'em, join 'em. So why don't you turn out for soccer and be on the team with Boyd and me?"

"Maybe I should. It would make Max happy. He's convinced I'm shutting myself off from my peer group."

"Great," said Lou, "let's go talk to Coach."

"On second thought," said Marcia, "maybe I'd be happier if I stayed depressed and bored."

I gave her the speech on depression that she had given me once. She threw her dill pickle at me. The bell rang, and as we got up, I grabbed Marcia's hand.

"I think I understand too," I said.

"It's not your fault," she said. Then we looked at each other as if we were seeing each other differently from before.

Lou yelled, "Save the passion for the dance. We're going to be late."

I thought I'd tell you about the game. The funny thing is I don't remember it all that clearly. I can't remember what people said during the game or even what the temperature was. It was like I was there but I wasn't all there. I sort of took things in but I didn't register a whole lot.

Weird. I remember feeling real weird on the field. Me in my too-big shorts and hairless legs. I was also pretty excited but I was trying not to be. I thought if I acted too excited I'd be labeled more out of it than I already was.

I kept telling myself it was just a game, and that finally worked about halfway through. About then I seemed to relax and just play. This was supposed to be for fun. I mean, it was just a practice game, not even the real thing. I think I enjoyed it a little, but I'm not sure.

Besides my strange feelings about the whole thing, it wasn't what you'd call an exciting game. The other team didn't even score. We scored once, and Lou was the one who did it. She said she had a little help from her friends.

The goal happened pretty soon after I loosened up. Jack passed me the ball, and I nudged it over to Lou, who slammed it past the goalie.

What's neat is that Lou was the hero. Coach Sandwich said she was going to be the captain of the team for the next game. Lou felt great. I felt great for her.

Marcia said to me after the game, "I told you Lou could handle things by herself just fine."

"Well, who do you suppose passed her the ball? You can't be a team all by yourself."

Then Marcia kissed me. It was just on the cheek, but she definitely kissed me. A real live kiss, and it felt fabulous. I felt my face getting hot and something weird was going on in my stomach. I looked at her, and I thought she was the most beautiful person I'd ever seen.

"I'm sorry," she said casually. "I know we're both dependent on you."

"I'm dependent on you, too," I said, but I was thinking how much I'd like to kiss her. Later tonight at the dance, I told myself. My jockstrap was getting tight. It was the only time I was glad my shorts were too big.

Marcia then let a bomb fall. "Do you still want to go to the dance with me?"

"Yes, of course. Why do you even ask?"

"Because Lou isn't going with us."

"What's wrong?" I asked.

"She's got another date."

"You've got to be kidding! With who?"

"Jack just asked her."

That guy doesn't give up. "You're kidding. Why did she say yes?" I asked, although I knew Lou probably thought it would make her mother happy.

"She said she wanted to give us a chance to be a couple for once without having a third

wheel around. She said three's a crowd sometimes."

Lou knew! She knew I was falling in love
with Marcia, probably before I even knew.

"She said," Marcia continued, "to tell you to
make it good because it would be our last date.
After this it's back to a good old threesome."

Well, maybe Lou didn't know exactly but
sensed something was going on. Now I was
scared. A real date. Marcia and me at a school
dance.

"Pick me up at 8:30," she said, "so we can
walk. I don't want my parents or yours to drive
us. Is that okay?"

"Right," I said. "I'll pick you up at 8:30."

All of a sudden I felt like we were strangers.
I couldn't talk to her anymore.

Marcia knew something was wrong, and as
we walked away, she said, "We're still friends
you know."

We're still friends all right and I'm going to
kiss my best friend tonight. I wondered what
Jack had up his sleeve. He couldn't be doing this
straight.

15

I ran all the way home. Being alive felt good. Everything works out if you let it. Lou scores the winning and only goal of the game, and I'm going to the dance with Marcia.

I wondered if Marcia's parents would act differently toward me now. I mean, maybe they would think things are different now that we are dating without Lou. You can bet they'll think differently about my being in Marcia's bedroom.

On second thought, I don't think it will make any difference. Why should it? Besides, Max isn't the type to pull quick changes like that. My parents maybe, but not Max.

Dinner felt like it took forever to eat, but by the time we finished, it was only 7:00 P.M. I was getting pretty excited. How would I ever make it to 8:30?

At dinner we talked about the game. My dad had come to watch me, and he said he was proud of me. I was glad he didn't say, "I didn't know you had it in you."

He said he was proud of the job I did and I actually believed him. My mom wasn't able to make it; she had given a talk at the library about photography.

Her talk hadn't gone all that well, and she was still kind of edgy about it. I was nervous about the dance. When she asked me what I was going to wear, I said, without thinking, "None of your business."

She threatened me with, "If you can't act civil, then maybe you'd better stay home tonight."

"I can act civil. I promise."

"We'll see about that," my dad said.

When they do that, it just drives me nuts. They always hold it over me. They keep me hanging. It'll be 8:25 and then, and only then, will they make up their minds. In the meantime, I will go absolutely berserk.

When I have kids, I'm never going to keep them waiting on a decision. I'm going to decide things far enough in advance so that they don't go nuts waiting. I promise you I'll never say, "We'll see."

I went upstairs, got ready, sat in my room and waited. When 8:15 rolled around, I casually walked downstairs and into the living room where my folks were watching TV.

"Well?" I asked.

"Well, what?" my mother said.

"Do I get to go or not?"

"Of course. What are you talking about?"

I could have pulled my hair out. Parents really do drive me crazy. It's no wonder junior high kids act like they are in an insane asylum. Their parents have made them totally nuts.

They say one thing and then a half hour later they say the opposite. If you asked me, I could give you the exact reason teenage suicide is on the rise. Parents.

Marcia says to get used to it. She thinks that it's probably what being an adult is all about.

You say and do one thing one day. Then you say and do the exact opposite thing the next day.

I left the house very quickly. I got out without even being asked what time I'd be in. I also got out without my coat and I should've worn a coat. It was starting to get cold. What did I think it was, still summer?

On the way to Marcia's house I practiced what I'd say to get her to kiss me again.

I tried, "How about a little kiss?" and "You wanna makeout?" but neither of the two seemed to fit the situation.

Maybe I should just forget it. We'd already kissed once today. Maybe she doesn't want to kiss me again. Maybe I've got bad breath. So I tell myself, if things don't work out, it'll be no big deal. All I have to do is act natural. Too bad I don't know what that is.

I pictured myself in the locker room after soccer practice. I have tons of pubic hair and someone asks me how my date was Saturday night. I tell them how fantastic it was and how we kissed forever.

I tripped over the crack in the sidewalk which brought me to my senses. What a dumb daydream. I remembered Marcia saying, "We're still friends," as I knocked on her door.

MARCIA opened the door and she looked great. I couldn't help it. I was in love. Can seventh graders get married?

We held hands, walking to the dance. We sort of talked funny at first, but pretty soon we loosened up and it was just a regular old time.

We got to the dance and the first thing we did was scout around for Lou and Jack. I thought I saw Jack in a corner but I couldn't see Lou.

We danced a couple of times while Mr. Sandwich was running around trying to get everyone to mix. Marcia explained to him that cakes were for mixing, not people. Like I said, that guy has no sense of humor. He gave us a dirty look and went and sat in a corner with some of the parents.

I said to Marcia, "I know that's Jack in the corner."

"Are you sure? Then where's Lou?"

"That's what I'd like to know," I said.

"Do you suppose he pulled something? Why don't you go over and ask him where she is?"

"Are you kidding?" I began to think we were about to have our first fight since we'd been on a dating basis.

"How about if we both go?"

Now how sensible. We avoided fighting. It would be much easier. We could just be a couple of friends, wondering where Jack hid our friend's body after he murdered her. Marcia did the talking.

"Hi, Jack." I thought she said it a little too friendly. "Where's Lou?"

"Oh, she couldn't make it."

"Ya," said his gooney friend, Greg, standing next to him. "She couldn't make it. She didn't feel good."

"That's too bad," said Marcia.

We walked away.

"Something's going on," I said. "We'd better go call her house."

Marcia went and got permission from Mr. Sandwich to use the faculty phone. The rule is no one, absolutely no one, uses the faculty phone. I'm not even sure the faculty get to use it. The only thing I can figure out is that Marcia must have used a couple of big words she had saved up to get herself to the library.

"How'd you do it?"

"Oh, it's easy. I'll teach you sometime."

I knew I'd like that.

Marcia dialed Lou's number. I had to watch from the hall because the two of us couldn't be alone in the room together. The world is sure that if you put a junior high boy and girl in the same room, they are going to jump all over each other.

I could see Marcia's mouth moving but I couldn't hear anything over the music in the gym. She didn't look happy. After only three minutes she came out.

"Well?"

"She's at the dance."

"She's not at the dance."

"I know. Her mother says she's at the dance."

"Now what do we do?" I asked.

"Go talk to Jack. Do you still know how to slug him in the gut? Because if you have forgotten, I'm going to learn how real fast."

Jack the Jerk, here I come.

I found him in the rest room. He and his gang of friends were passing a joint around. Counting Jack, there were four of them.

"Well, if it isn't the guy with the two girls," said Jack.

"What happened to Lou?"

"I told you she got sick."

"We called her place and her mother said she was here."

"I don't see her unless she's in one of the stalls. Why don't you smoke some of this and you won't be so weird," Jack said as he offered me the joint.

"No, thanks," I said. "Where's Lou?"

"She ain't here I told you. Maybe she didn't feel like coming."

They all looked at me. What was I supposed to do now? Beat them all up? If Lou could take care of herself, I wished she'd hurry up and do it.

I left as quickly as I could.

WE figured there was nothing we could do right then. Marcia said calling the cops or Lou's parents would only get Lou in trouble. It didn't look as if I could convince Jack to tell me what was going on. The only thing we could do was wait.

"Lou's a strong young woman. She can take care of herself." I couldn't help but throw that quote back at Marcia.

She started to slug me, then changed her mind and kissed me again. This time I kissed her back. No big deal. I just put my mouth close to hers and let it happen.

We danced a couple of fast songs and a real nice slow one. Jack came up to us and tried to cut in. I looked at Marcia and said, "It's up to you."

She calmly told Jack to stuff it in his ear.

He started laughing real loud and screamed, "You think you're hot stuff, don't you? The three of you are real freaks, you know."

At that point people around us stopped dancing. Someone told Jack to shut up or the chaperones would come over.

"You're the freak," I said to him.

Marcia said, "Stop it. I'm not going to be a part of a name-calling match."

Jack started to yell something else when Lou walked in. She was wearing a dress, or rather it was wearing her. It was ripped along the bottom and dirty at the edges.

I thought there were going to be fireworks; she looked so hurt and mad. She acted like she wanted to say something, but she just stood there looking at Jack.

One of Jack's friends said, "Well, look what the cat dragged in."

Lou looked over at him, then back at Jack. Then Lou cried. She stood there and sobbed. I noticed she had a wilted flower in her hair. It was horrible. I felt like crying.

Marcia put her arms around Lou. I sort of stood there getting lost in feeling sad that this was happening. I looked at Jack. His eyes were fixed on the floor.

We left. Lou was between us still crying. We walked to Marcia's house and sat on the floor of the greenhouse.

It was a good place. It was warm, and the feel of the plants all around us was comforting. We sat there talking. Lou cried some more, and then she told us what happened.

They, Jack and one of his friends who was in high school, had picked her up in his friend's car. They took her out in the country about eight miles and then told her to get out of the car.

"I didn't know what to do," said Lou. "I could have slugged him, but I was so embarrassed. I had really thought he wanted to go out with me. I thought he liked me. What an idiot I am. I'd put on a dress. I put a flower behind my ear. You should have seen my mother. She was so proud of me. What could I do? I got out of the car and walked to the school. I feel so hurt. What will I tell my parents?"

"What you'll tell them is the truth," said Marcia, "and then your dad will beat Jack to a bloody pulp. No, better yet, we'll sue. We'll have him arrested for kidnapping. We'll get him thrown in jail and throw away the key. We'll get a lawyer who will go for the death penalty. It would serve him right. God, I hate him."

Lou said, "I can't tell my parents. It will just kill them. I'll just tell them I played football on the way home. I know; I'll tell them I fell in a mud puddle and got run over by a truck."

"They're sure to believe that," I said, carefully picking the wilted flower out of Lou's hair.

Marcia said to me, "I'm glad you're not like Jack."

I was glad I wasn't like Jack, too.

Marcia told Lou, "You should have broken his arm."

We laughed a little, and then went into the kitchen and had root-beer floats. Later I kissed both Lou and Marcia on the cheek and went home.

WHEN I got home my mom and dad asked me if I had a good time at the dance. I said, "Sure, it was okay."

Mom said, "Well, what happened?"

I said, "Oh, it was just a dance." What was I supposed to say? Tell them that Lou had been kidnapped, that I can't believe what a jerk Jack is, and that I think I'm more in love with Marcia now than ever?

I turned on the TV, but I couldn't concentrate. I felt too crummy. I felt sorry for myself.

I felt sorry for Lou, and I felt sorry for every kid who had to go through puberty and junior high all at the same time, because it's pretty damn awful becoming an adult sometimes.

A commercial came on. This woman was all upset because her husband never asked for a second helping of frozen peas when she fixed them, but at the neighbor's house he did. She was trying to find out from the neighbor the brand of frozen peas she cooked.

I screamed at the set, "Who cares! He asked for seconds to be polite. He really hates frozen peas."

It killed me. They acted like they had never talked to each other before in their lives. They needed to be introduced to each other. He was so stupid that he couldn't tell his wife he didn't like the kind of frozen peas she bought. And she was so stupid that she cared.

I figured out in that moment what it means to be a man. It means you spend your time trying to make women guess what you want out of life and what kind of frozen peas you prefer. I feel sorry for the whole world. No wonder Jack is such a moron.

I should call Jack up and tell him what a jerk he truly is and how he had a chance to really get to know a great person that just happens to be a girl. I'd probably be wasting my time.

It's so depressing. What if the world is full of Jack's who believe all the rules about what you do and act like if you're a boy or girl. What if it's full of people who care about frozen peas?

There's a chance, however, that the world has at least a couple more Lou's and Marcia's in it. I guess there's still hope.

Hey, I just looked at myself in the mirror, and I think I need to shave.

Thanks, Marcia, for kissing me. It has to be the nicest thing that ever happened to me—so far.